Zac Runs Wild
published in 2014 by
Hardie Grant Egmont
Ground Floor, Building 1, 658 Church Street
Richmond, Victoria 3121, Australia
www.hardiegrantegmont.com.au

A CiP record for this title is available from the National Library of
Australia.

Illustrations by Tomomi Sarafov
Design by Stephanie Spartels
Zac Power logo design by Simon Swingler

Printed in Australia by McPherson's Printing Group, Maryborough,
Victoria, an accredited ISO AS/NZS 14001 Environmental
Management System printer.

5 7 9 10 8 6 4

The paper this book is printed on is certified against
the Forest Stewardship Council® Standards. FSC®
promotes environmentally responsible, socially beneficial
and economically viable management of the world's
forests.

ZAC RUNS WILD

BY H.I. LARRY

ILLUSTRATIONS BY TOMOMI SARAFOV

hardie grant EGMONT

CHAPTER

Zac Power was at school.

It was lunch time. He was

playing cricket with his friends.

Zac was 12 years old, but he

wasn't like other kids.

Zac was a new Spy Recruit.
His code name was Agent
Rock Star.

Zac worked for a good spy
group called GIB.

Sometimes GIB sent Zac to
Spy Camp. He learnt cool spy
skills like rock-climbing there.

'You're up, Zac,' called one of
Zac's friends.

Zac walked to the crease.

The bowler threw the ball
at him.

Zac hit the ball for six.

Wow, this bat is powerful,
thought Zac. He looked
closely at the bat. There was
a message on it.

**PRESS HERE TO GO TO
SPY CAMP.**

'I'll be back soon,' called Zac.
He ran behind a classroom.

Zac pressed the button on
the cricket bat.

Four turbo wheels popped out.

It looked like a skateboard.

Zac put the bat on the ground
and jumped on. The bat
zoomed away by itself.

CHAPTER

Zac rode his cricket bat down the street. Soon he arrived at the big silver Spy Camp dome.

He went inside. There was a girl waiting at the front desk. She was using a SpyPad.

Every GIB spy had a SpyPad.
It was a smart phone and a
mini tablet. Zac had music,
games and a laser on his.

Zac got his Info-Disk from
the front desk.

It had his Spy Camp

information on it.

Zac put it into his SpyPad.

A message popped up.

Spy Camp Skill:
Animal Handling

Training Buddy:
Agent Fang

Training Place:
Jungle Base

Cool, thought Zac. He hadn't met Agent Fang.

'Excuse me,' said the girl at the desk. 'Do you know Agent Rock Star?'

'That's me,' said Zac.

'Great!' said the girl. 'I'm Agent Fang. My real name is Anna.'

'Cool code name,' said Zac. 'My real name is Zac. Let's go!'

They walked across the dome.
Zac looked up. A huge screen
showed the Spy Ladder results.

Every week spies got points for
missions and Spy Camp tests.
Spies with lots of points went
to the top of the ladder. This
week Zac was number one.

There were doors all around the
edge of the Spy Camp dome.

They led to rooms full of Spy Camp training gear.

Zac and Anna found the Animal Handling door. Zac scanned his SpyPad over the lock. The door opened.

There was a vehicle inside that looked like a snake.

'This vehicle is rad!' said Anna. 'I love snakes. In fact, I love all animals.'

They took a closer look.

It was a Speed Snake.

The snake had metal scales

and two big windows for eyes.

Suddenly the mouth opened.

It was the Speed Snake's door.

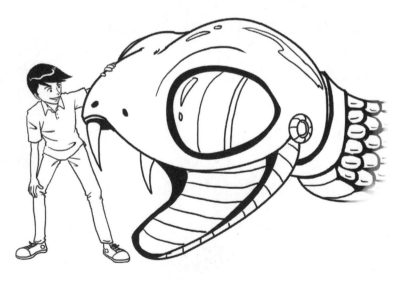

Anna opened a roller door at the back of the room.

Zac picked up two boxes from a shelf. 'Let's go,' he said.

Zac crawled inside the Speed Snake's mouth. Anna followed.

Zac turned the key and sped out through the roller door.

CHAPTER

Zac and Anna drove for ages.

Zac turned on auto-pilot.

Then he opened one of the

gadget boxes.

There was a belt inside.

It had a star-shaped buckle.

There was one for Anna too.

They put them on.

Soon the Speed Snake slowed

down and then stopped.

'I think we're here,' said Zac.

Zac and Anna crawled out of

the Speed Snake's mouth.

Zac looked around. They were

in a thick jungle.

Suddenly, something flew towards them. It was a man swinging on a vine. He landed in front of Zac and Anna.

'Welcome to Animal Training,' said the man.

'I'm Agent Tarzan. Today you'll learn about dangerous animals. Then you'll be tested.'

Agent Tarzan was carrying two backpacks. He gave them to Anna and Zac.

'These are full of food,' said Agent Tarzan. 'Sometimes you can use food to get past unfriendly animals.'

Zac and Anna put on the backpacks.

Agent Tarzan pulled on a branch. A tree trunk opened up. A screen popped out.

'This is the Animal Tracker computer,' said Agent Tarzan.

He touched the computer screen. A picture of two birds popped up.

'Which bird might attack you?' asked Agent Tarzan.

Zac thought for a second. But Anna spoke up straight away.

'The pretty one,' said Anna.
'That's the male bird. He wants
to protect his home.'

'Well done,' said Agent Tarzan.

Zac saw that he would have to
be fast to keep up with Anna.

Next, a big lizard came up on
the screen.

'Touch the lizard's skin, Zac,'
said Agent Tarzan.

Zac ran his hand over the screen. It felt **SCALY**.

'Wow,' said Zac. 'It feels like real lizard skin!'

'You can pat animals on the Animal Tracker,' said Agent Tarzan. 'But sometimes you shouldn't pat them in real life.'

Anna and Zac spent ages on the Animal Tracker.

Anna knew lots already but Zac learnt super fast.

'It's time for your test,' said Agent Tarzan.

'Bring it on!' said Zac.

CHAPTER

'Your test is a race through

the jungle,' said Agent Tarzan.

He pointed to two paths

through the jungle. 'You have

to get past lots of animals.

You'll take different paths.
But you'll end up in the same
place. Your score will give you
Spy Ladder points.'

'Good luck,' said Anna to Zac.

'You too,' said Zac.

'Ready, set, GO!' said Agent
Tarzan.

Zac and Anna raced into the
jungle on the two paths.

After a few minutes, Zac saw
an elephant up ahead.

I'll give him some food, thought
Zac. *Maybe he'll let me past.*
He took some bananas out of
his backpack. Then he walked
up to the elephant.

The elephant reached out its
trunk and took the bananas.

Zac tip-toed around the
elephant. He turned a corner.

There was a huge spider web across the path!

Zac stopped just in time.
He saw something move in the corner of the web. It was a giant hairy spider. It was bigger than Zac's backpack!

He looks nasty, thought Zac.
He carefully ducked under without touching the web.

It was like crossing a laser trap.
Zac had gone through laser
traps lots of times.

Zac started running. He passed lots of animals. He knew what to do every time.

Zac reached the finish line. There were two buttons there. He pressed his button to show he had finished.

Anna was nowhere to be seen. Zac leant against a tree to wait for her.

Soon, Zac saw Anna coming
towards him. She was carrying
a lion cub!

'What are you doing?'
asked Zac.

'The cub was lost,' said Anna.

'And now it thinks I'm its

mother.'

Suddenly,

ROAR! ROAR!

Zac saw a mother lion on the

path behind Anna. And it did

not look happy.

CHAPTER 5

Zac stayed very still.

Anna put the cub on the ground, but it jumped back into her arms.

'It won't let go!' said Anna.

The mother lion came towards Zac and Anna.

'Just run, Anna!' Zac shouted.

They turned and ran. Zac looked back. The mother lion was catching up fast!

Suddenly, Zac had an idea.

'Let's cross the river,' said Zac. 'We can plan our next move once we're across. This way!'

Zac and Anna turned off the path and they ran through the bushes. Zac could see the river.

'Now!' yelled Zac. He aimed his Shooting Star belt at a branch above the river.
He pressed the button and the star shot out. It stuck to the branch. Zac swung across the river on the rope.

Zac landed on his feet. Anna
swung across too. The lion
cub held on to her back.

When Anna landed, she fell over.
Her backpack ripped open.

The food went everywhere.

The cub jumped down to the food. It picked up a piece of meat and started eating it.

'Hang on,' said Anna. 'The cub just wanted food!'

'I wonder if the mother lion is hungry too,' said Zac. 'We can distract her with food, like Agent Tarzan said.'

'It's worth a try,' said Anna.

She put the cub in her backpack. They swung back across the river.

Zac made sure they were a little way away from the mother lion.

Zac got a piece of meat out of his backpack. He threw it towards the mother lion.

She caught it in her mouth

and sat down to eat it.

The cub jumped out of Anna's

backpack. It ran over and

started eating the meat as well.

'Aww, they're so sweet,'
said Anna.

Zac laughed. 'They weren't
sweet a minute ago!' he said.
'Come on, let's get back.'

CHAPTER

Anna and Zac ran back to the finish line. Agent Tarzan was waiting for them.

'Where have you been?' asked Agent Tarzan.

'We met a cute lion cub,' said Anna.

'And a mother lion who was totally not cute,' said Zac.

Agent Tarzan laughed. 'I'm glad you're OK,' he said. 'You can head back to Spy Camp now.'

Zac and Anna drove the Speed Snake back to Spy Camp. When they got back they went straight to the canteen.

'I'm starving,' said Zac. 'I'm going to have special chicken and then chocolate mousse.'

A message came through on Zac's SpyPad. Anna's SpyPad beeped as well. It was their test results.

Zac read his message.

Super speedy and top animal skills.

10 points.

Zac was still number one on the Spy Ladder.

'I only got five points,' said Anna. 'They said I should remember that baby animals can have scary mums!'

'Oh, well,' said Zac. 'We did get chased by a lion. That's pretty cool!'

'You're right,' said Anna. 'I can't wait to tell the other agents!'

THE END